SMILE OUT LOUD

INTRODUCTION

A SMILE IS INFECTIOUS — TRY IT AND SEE!

When you smile, other people smile back, and just like that people
start catching smiles. Some of those smiles might turn into giggles,
chuckles and even big old belly laughs — you just never know.
I've written these poems to help you spread some happiness.

Some poems involve doing silly walks, some have you pulling silly faces,
and there are even some that will get all your mords in a wuddle!
So take care, you may find that these poems lead to you and
your friends rolling on the floor in a riot of whoops and chortles.

There are poems here for you to perform alone, with friends,
and in large groups. There are all sorts of performance techniques
to try out, too. However you perform these poems, remember the
biggest rule of all... poetry is fun and ultimately there are no rules.

You can shout a poem intended to be whispered, read a group poem
by yourself, or add actions to a tongue twister. You can mix up and
dip into the different performance techniques whenever you want.
So let's get started — jump in and start performing
your poems OUT LOUD!

THE LAUGH

This poem is all about laughter starting as a little giggle and ending up taking over your entire body. Start reading with a small smile and make it bigger as you go. Then see if you can bring a little bit of chuckling into your voice. How far can you take it? Will you end up rolling on the floor laughing?

It started as a tickle
as a wriggle on my lips.
It turned into a giggle,
a wiggle of the hips.

It turned into a jitter,
a titter of the teeth.
My face is turning red
and it's begging for release.

It gasps into a guffaw!
Into a great big belly laugh.
If I whoop any louder
"Call the security staff!"

Now it's spreading to my friends
in snickers, chuckles and snorts.
If we roar any louder
we'll get a school report!

Now our sides are splitting!
We're on the floor laughing!

We cannot stop!
We will not stop!
It's threatening to choke!

And all because of the telling
of a wonderfully silly joke.

WALKING FUNNY

These poems are instructions for some
funny walks to make you smile.
Can you perfect the walks
and memorise the poems?

THE DINOSAUR

Pull your trousers up
as far as they will go,
stick your bottom out
and walk like a chicken,
            walk like a chicken,
            walk like a chicken,
a finger-licking chicken.

But instead of clucking –
clucking while you're ducking,
let yourself roar!
            Like a dinosaur,
            like a dinosaur,
a roar-dinosaur!

THE BALLERINA

Stand on tiptoe
arms out in front
holding an imaginary belly,
Now turn!
Now spin!
Now leap!
and...
Plié! Plié! Petit
Jeté
flutter and glide
the day away.

THE SLOW-MO

Walk through egg yolks.
egg-aggerate your movements.

Let your strides become a slog – sloth slow.
Let the sloth-slow, slow-mo spread
(sluggish-slug-slow)
to your arms and head.

Watch as your face
clunks and gears
like drying paint
as time winds down.

ZEUGMAS

A zeugma is a word used to link two things or ideas at once – for example,
"When she tripped me at the Valentine's dance, she **broke** my leg and my heart".
This is a poem full of zeugmas! See if you can make up some zeugmas of your own.

When I went fishing
I **caught** a cod and a cold.
The cold got me coughing
and the cod felt pretty cold.

During the race
my nose and trainers **ran**!
I got through a box of tissues
before the race even began.

On holiday
I **surfed** the waves and the web.
It was hard to get Wi-Fi
with my laptop on my head.

At the pick 'n' mix
I **picked** some candy and my nose.
My fingers got pretty sticky,
so I ate the candy with my toes!

At the fair
I **lost** my temper and my phone.
I never found my temper
but I heard a few ring tones.

In the dark forest
the wind and the wolves **howled**.
The wind whisked itself away
whenever those wolves growled.

In the jungle
I **fell** into a hole and a bad mood.
The hole was full of angry beasts
that wouldn't share their food!

IMAGINATION RUNNING FREE

When reading this poem out loud, invite your audience to close their eyes
and imagine the different scenes that the poem creates.
But be warned, the poem has a silly ending!

Close your eyes
what do you see?
imagination running free.

Imagine your toes
in a gentle sea.
Imagination running free.

Imagine your legs
are two conker trees!
Imagination running free.

Imagine your knees
are stripy like bees!
imagination running free.

Imagine you're running with:
  toes wet
  legs wooden
  knees stripy!

That's your imagination
  running free.

MONSTROUS FACES

This poem is best read in a mirror. Each verse describes a different monstrous face.
See if you can pull each face after reading each verse. Warning… may cause giggling.

Faces can be screwed up
scrunched up
or even mean.
Stick your top teeth
on your bottom lip
and you're a blood-sucking fiend.

Faces can be wide-open
closed-shut
or even scrunched!
Close your eyelids tight,
touch nose to lips
and you're a witch hungry for lunch.

Faces can be inflated,
deflated
or even cadaverous.
Suck in your cheeks
and widen your eyes
and you're a ghoul feeling cantankerous!

Faces can be shocked,
surprised
or even terrified!
Look in the mirror
and be surprised
by all the faces
that your face hides!

I SPY

This game of 'I Spy' is a bit different…
At the end of this poem, carry on with your own silly 'I Spy' phrases.
See what strange sentences you can create with these body parts:
cheek, belly, fist, elbow, neck, lap, hair and back!

I spy
with my little eye.

I hear
with my little ear.

A song is sung
with my little tongue.

I tell the truth
with my little tooth.

I balance a boulder
on my little shoulder.

I conduct a band
with my little hand.

I pick up a singer
with my little finger.

There's a clothes peg
on my little leg.

I trip over a root
with my little foot.

I smell my toes
with my little nose.

I place the sea
on my little knee.

THE DRAGGING DRAGON

This poem uses a lot of repetition. Invite your audience to join you in the reading of this poem. Tell them to say "dragged on behind him" whenever you give them a visual cue. This cue could be as simple as pointing at them when you want them to say it. Having the extra voices joining you at the end of each verse will help bring the rhythm of the poem to life.

There was a dragon
with a very long
very bothersome tail
and it dragged-on behind him.

His tail was long,
long and thin
and it dragged-on behind him.

He dragged it over mountains
where the moss-rocks turned it green.
as it dragged-on behind him.

He dragged it through the forests
where leaves caught in his tail's scales
as it dragged-on behind him.

He dragged it through wildflower fields
where the pollen speckled it bright
as it dragged-on behind him.

He dragged it between the cities' shops
where it tangled around buns and ladies' frocks!
As it dragged-on behind him.

14

There was a dragon
with a very long,
very wonderful tail
that he would curl all around him

A tail soft with the mountain's moss,
a tail sheaved with the forest's leaves,
a tail that had thrust through a flower's dust,
a tail that had shopped a city's shops,
and the dragon curled it up around him.

He curled it up,
his wonderful tail
the dragon curled it up
around him.

SPACE IS....

Use your whole body when reading this poem.
Can you show just how big space is?
Try spreading your arms, widening your legs,
moving in all directions, taking up as much
space as you can. And remember,
it will be easiest to do this if you can
memorise the poem first.

Space is high
and large
and wide and black and star-filled
and we are in it.

Space is big
and deep
and long and empty and planet-peppered
and we are in it.

Space is above
and below
and inside and outside and galaxy-salted
and we are in it.

Space is slow
and fast
and bumpy and odd and spaceship-filled
and we are speeding through it.

And the quicker we go
the slower we grow
and the faster we speed
the faster all else runs to seed.

For space is strange
and weird
and wonderful and Home and adventure-packed
and we are in it.

AS I WALKED

This poem was inspired by a walk.
Next time you go for a walk, try noting what you see.
Maybe you can write a poem about your walk –
use the first line from each verse (in bold)
as the starting point for each verse in your poem.

As I walked, I wondered

about the tree about to be cut down
a universe of living things
strewn harshly on the ground.

As I walked, I pondered

on the house where the family would shout
the skips carrying their pain away
where could they be right now?

As I walked, I grimaced

at the rubbish on the ground
it seems to be getting worse
making a mess of our little town.

As I walked, I marvelled
at the sea's endless invite
I saw the surfers riding its waves –
waves of escape, waves of delight.

As I walked, I heard
families laughing on the sands
dogs racing wildly
children building imaginary lands.

As I walked, I saw
a lady in her chair
struggling down the bumpy road –
her dog's protective stare.

My walks make me wonder
of the variety of life
the sadness and the joy
the leisure and the strife.

The pain that some endure
while others whizz on by
the world we must protect
while we're all just trying to get by.

So, a resolution forms
starts walking through my head
to remove all judgment
all pointless point and blame
to choose another way, a kinder, gentler route
through life's ambling game.

WHEN SADNESS COMES

Perform this poem in a group. Divide up the verses
between you, and take it in turns to read them.
When one person is reading, the others can enact
the scene around them – pretending to listen to music,
dancing, watching birds in the sky.

When sadness comes and finds me
and hope seems far away
and everything feels inside out
and grey clouds consume my day.

I turn the radio on
and listen to a favourite tune
the music explodes within me
I'll be smiling soon.

Or I take out some paper
and a kaleidoscope of pens
I dream and doodle my blues away
and watch the sadness end.

Or I dance like I'm on telly
with cameras all around
doing all my signature moves
and then my smile astounds.

Or I head out on to the balcony
and watch the birds up in the sky
their aerial acrobatics
makes my smile touch my eyes.

Or I talk to a friend
about the rumblings inside
their listening warms me
and my smile feels ten feet wide.

All these little things I do
whenever sadness comes a-knocking
and through the sadness I soon find
a smile soon comes a-rocking.

RECIPE FOR THIS BOY

Get a friend to help you with this poem. Ask them to act out all the baking
actions, like mixing ingredients in a bowl and adding a dash of bravery.
Maybe they could do the actions around you as you read,
so it's like they are making you!

Take two cried-out eyes,
a pinch of loneliness,
mix in a bowl.

Add a dash of bravery,
two heaped teaspoons of brotherly love,
fold in fear.

Crack a box of giggles,
beat into stomach-aching guffaws,
blend until smooth.

Add a cup of heart,
pour in three thick handfuls of hair,
knead with tickling fingers.

Roll out onto a city pavement
egg-frying hot with summer heat,
cookie cut the shape of a boy.

Decorate with giggles,
dust with smiling tears,
leave to rise
under the heat of a happy sun.

A BRUSH WITH DANGER

This poem has a surprise at the end - it's written by a yeti!
Try experimenting with your voice as you read.
Start out talking like yourself, then by the end of the poem go full yeti!
What does a yeti sound like, I wonder?

Dad likes to brush his hair
Dad likes to brush his teeth
Dad likes to brush his eyebrows,
his eyebrows! Good grief

Dad likes to brush his arms
and the hair upon his back
Dad likes to brush each hairy leg,
now what do you think of that!

Dad likes to brush his toes
and his ever-so-hairy tongue,
Dad likes to brush the bridge of his nose
and his cheeks, just for fun.

Dad's always leaving hair
in trails across the floor
and not one plug within our home
flows with water anymore.

Because Dad is a yeti
and I'm a yeti too,
we're great big hairy yetis
and we're coming to brush you!

YOU COULD, YOU WOULD, AWAKE A DINOSAUR

This type of poem is called a villanelle.
It has regular repeating lines and rhymes, and it is perfect to read with friends.
Divide up the blue lines among you and read the yellow lines together.

You could, you would, awake a dinosaur
from the museum's pile of dusty bones –

Sing a song of bone with a mighty roar.

My song was a dream, dreamed on the museum's floor,
at a museum sleepover, far from home.

You could, you would, awake a dinosaur.

My dream got loud, got ready to soar,
an old jawbone jiggled and giggled and groaned.

Sing a song of bone with a mighty roar.

Each bone did a shuffle over the floor.
My song of dream was tooth and claw and bone.

You could, you would, awake a dinosaur.

Then scales and skin grew on the dinosaur,
it whispered to me in the softest tone.

"Please sing my song of bone, with a mighty roar."

And so, we boomed across the shaking floor,
the marble steps made the perfect throne.

You could, you would, awake a dinosaur,
just sing a song of bone with a mighty roar.

DADA'S TREASURES

This is a poem to be acted. You can act the whole poem by yourself,
taking the roles of the grandchild and Dada, or perform it with a friend.
The grandchild's lines are in green bubbles and
Dada's lines are in orange bubbles.

Dada's shed was OUT OF BOUNDS
for that was where he kept his treasure.

"Stay out of my shed
It's where I keep my treasure."

Dada was snoozing
in his small round brown chair
with his rusted shed key
dangling from his pocket.

"Stay out of my shed
It's where I keep my treasure."

I picked the key
slowly,
so slowly,
slower than a flower blooming.

"Stay out of my shed
It's where I keep my treasure."

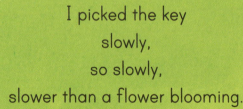

I crawled up to his dark shed...
Unlock!
Lift-catch!
Squeak door!

"Stay out of my shed
It's where I keep my treasure."

Dada has shot up
from his small brown round chair
barking at me...

"STAY OUT OF MY SHED
IT'S WHERE I KEEP MY TREASURE!"

I stand behind Dada
as he picks his way between:
big things,
metal things,
sharp things,
deadly things!

"Stay out of my shed
only I can get the treasure!"

Dada opens his hands...
there are tomato seeds small as ladybird wings

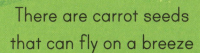

"These grow tomatoes
bigger than your head!"

There are carrot seeds
that can fly on a breeze

"These grow carrots of orange, yellow and red!"

There are pumpkin seeds,
each as thick as Dada's nails

"These grow pumpkins big enough to use as a bed!
These are my seeds
and these are my treasures."

MEMORIES OF SMILES

Happy memories can comfort us in difficult times.
To write this poem, I thought back to some of my happiest memories
and they made me smile. Share your happy memories with a friend
or classmate. Then try turning these memories into simple descriptions,
and build up your own poem.

Being tickled by my mum
until my cheeks ached
until my breath came out in snorts
until I gasped "stop"
even though I was loving every second.

From my bedroom window
of our flat at the peak of our tower,
my father's car is all aurora lights.
The cold press of the windows against my palms
felt impenetrable, like an Everest climb.

I wanted to trek to him,
to scale down the stairs to meet him
but I couldn't move
I needed to see what he was going to reveal
from his car's midnight depths...
A bike, a brand-new mountain bike.

The ferry to France on a school trip.
Sitting on deck with a splash of friends
using our pocket money
to buy salted crisps and mouth-melt chocolate
watching our home slide away,
watching new adventures roll up ahead.

Reading by the Christmas tree
as the night rolled in.
Letting the words snowfall in my mind
to the tinkling of the Christmas lights,
as tales of ghosts and plum puddings
unwrap their gifts.

I WOKE UP WITH A SMILE

This poem is all about dreams and what might cause them.
It's a type of poem called a rondel, which uses repeating lines and has two rhymes.
Each line in this poem rhymes with either 'head' or 'smile'.
Why not try keeping your own dream journal?
You can use it as inspiration for writing poems.

I woke up with a smile
as a dream tickled my head.
I dreamed I was a crocodile
and marshmallows were my bed.

Perhaps it was the book I read
that made my dreams go wild.
I woke up with a smile
as a dream tickled my head.
Or something that my brother said
as we went to bed.

Some little thing, that for a while
kept my fantasies well fed.
I woke up with a smile
as a dream tickled my head.

A TIP OF THE SLONGUE

This poem uses spoonerisms. A spoonerism is when you swap the first letters –
normally consonants (such as b, g, p, s), rather than vowels (a, e, i, o, u) –
of two words. I've had fun playing with spoonerisms in this poem.
Can you think of any more? Can you turn your spoonerisms into a poem?

Today I had a tip of the slongue
I mean a slip of the tongue.

I told my teacher,
"I'm so sorry, sir,
but my mords are all in a wuddle."

"Stop being so billy, soy," he said.
"You've got me noing it dow!"
And the whole class lurst out baughing.

"It's not my fault, sir," I said.
"I han't celp it!"

And now the whole class
are challing out of their fairs
and rolling on the loor flaughing.

"That's enough," said Sir.
"Any more and I'll send you to the Heputy Deadmaster.
It's not smart or clever,
you are not being a fart smeller!"

CRASHED TO THE GROUND

Repeating a word or phrase can be a great way to inject rhythm into your poems.
As you read this poem, use your voice to emphasise the repeating lines.
You could even get your audience to join in with the repeating bits.
Let's hope the things in this poem never happen to you!

Birthday cake
high on a table
Birthday cake
I think I'm able
Birthday cake
to get it down
Birthday cake
crashed to the ground!

Easter egg
up on the shelf
Easter egg
for no one else
Easter egg
I give it a go
Easter egg
standing on tiptoe
Easter egg
tumbles down
Easter egg
crashed to the ground!

Christmas present
under the bed
Christmas present
rolling round my head
Christmas present
I start to sneak
Christmas present
to have a peek
Christmas present
I lift it high
Christmas present
up to my eye
Christmas present
It makes a shocking sound
Christmas present
crashed to the ground!

FUN WITH ANIMAL NAMES

Try playing with the endings of some different animal names –
crocodile, octopus, platypus, rhinoceros, scorpion and orangutan –
and putting them in your own poem. When a platypus has a cold,
does it sneeze-ypus? Have fun and remember to smile-odile like a crocodile!

HIPPOPOT-AMUS

I know a hippopotamus
he sips from a teapot-amus
he's such a proper hippopotamus
he ties his tie with a Windsor knot-amus.

I know a hippopotamus
who won the jackpot-amus
and sails on his yacht-amus
such a lucky hippopotamus.

ARMADILL-O

I met an armadillo
who could never chill-o
spent her day on the treadmill-o
such a sporty armadillo.

I met an armadillo
who ran from here to Brazil-o
uphill and downhill-o
purely for the thrill-o.

I met an armadillo
a very tired armadillo
not moving, totally still-o
fast asleep on her pillow.

AYE-AYE

I once saw an aye-aye
such a creepy little aye-aye
staring at me with her eye-eye.
I left with a quick bye-bye.

Around every corner there's that aye-aye
she's following me, but why-why?
such a creepy little aye-aye
I wonder if she's a spy-spy?

I run around town as I try-try
to lose this private eye-eye
but wherever I go she's nearby-by
that creepy little aye-aye.

BEDTIME

This is a poem designed to be read just before bed.
So take a nice deep breath, feel all your muscles relax,
and read the poem in your most gentle calming voice.
Maybe you can read it to a family member
to help them snooze off to sleep.

Sleep upon the hours

that the darkness keeps.

Roll up in the minutes

that the moon slowly sighs.

Sink into the seconds

that the stars twinkle by.

Dream of the face

that makes you smile when you wake.

Snuffle in the song of chimes

from yawning hills when morning breaks.

Snuggle into tomorrow

with the sun's brightening dawn.

A world of wonder awaits you

what adventures will you go on?

For Gracie and Harrison – J.C.

For Taylem – D.G-B.

Brimming with creative inspiration, how-to projects, and useful information to enrich your everyday life, quarto.com is a favorite destination for those pursuing their interests and passions.

First published in 2022 by Wide Eyed Editions, an imprint of The Quarto Group.
The Old Brewery, 6 Blundell Street, London N7 9BH, United Kingdom.
T (0)20 7700 6700 F (0)20 7700 8066 www.Quarto.com

A catalogue record for this book is available from the British Library.

ISBN 978-0-7112-8456-2

The illustrations were created with traditional and digital media
Set in Nature Spirit, Bodoni and Print Clearly

Designed by Belinda Webster
Edited by Alice Harman
Commissioned by Lucy Brownridge
Production by Dawn Cameron
Published by Georgia Amson-Bradshaw

Manufactured in Guangdong, China TT112022

9 8 7 6 5 4 3 2 1